ON OUR WAY TO OYSTER BAY

MOTHER JONES

AND HER MARCH FOR CHILDREN'S RIGHTS

WRITTEN BY MONICA KULLING

ILLUSTRATED BY FELICITA SALA

Citizen**Kid** ™

A collection of books that inform children about the
world and inspire them to be better global citizens

KIDS CAN PRESS

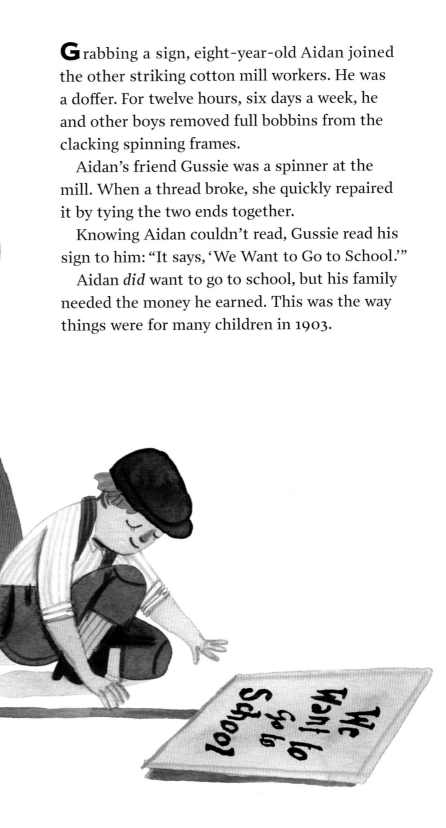

Grabbing a sign, eight-year-old Aidan joined the other striking cotton mill workers. He was a doffer. For twelve hours, six days a week, he and other boys removed full bobbins from the clacking spinning frames.

Aidan's friend Gussie was a spinner at the mill. When a thread broke, she quickly repaired it by tying the two ends together.

Knowing Aidan couldn't read, Gussie read his sign to him: "It says, 'We Want to Go to School.'"

Aidan *did* want to go to school, but his family needed the money he earned. This was the way things were for many children in 1903.

There was excitement on the picket line that day. Someone named Mother Jones was coming. She helped workers fight for better wages and safer working conditions.

When Aidan met her, though, he wondered how.

"She looks like someone's granny!" he whispered to Gussie.

Later, Aidan was even more surprised when Mother Jones talked his mam, and Gussie's, too, into letting them join a march from Kensington, Pennsylvania, to Oyster Bay, New York — over one hundred miles away!

In her travels, Mother Jones had met hundreds of children working in factories and mills. Many were missing fingers; some had even lost hands.

Troubled by all she had seen, Mother Jones wanted to end child labor. But what could she do? Why, organize a children's march and bring the message right to President Theodore Roosevelt at his summer home in Oyster Bay, of course!

A few days after arriving in Kensington, Mother Jones gathered two hundred workers, including an excited Aidan, Gussie and dozens of other children. They marched out of town playing flutes, beating drums and waving flags.

Mother Jones was leading the way to Oyster Bay!

The first day of the march seemed like it would never end, but Aidan and Gussie kept each other going. All the same, they were very happy when Mother Jones shouted, "Camp time!"

While the tents were being set up, Mother Jones helped some of the women make a large pot of meat-and-potato stew. It smelled heavenly.

Aidan and Gussie ate until they couldn't eat any more. And later, under a blanket of stars, they slept as soundly as hibernating bears.

The days were long and hot, and the mosquitoes were biting. Each day a few of the marchers quit. But not Aidan and Gussie. They enjoyed walking through fields of buttercups and visiting new towns. And it felt good to be doing something so important.

Besides, if old Mother Jones could walk this far, why couldn't they?

Aidan wasn't the only one in the group who couldn't read. At the end of each day, Mother Jones read the daily news aloud in her soothing Irish lilt. Some of the stories were even about the march!

The march wasn't all buttercups and sunshine, though. One day the rain fell in torrents, making the dirt roads sloppy with thick mud. By nightfall, Aidan and Gussie were exhausted.

Somehow Mother Jones convinced the mayor of the next town to let the marchers spend that night in an empty meeting hall. Soaked to the skin, everyone was grateful for a dry place to rest and a dinner of cold sandwiches.

"She's something!" whispered Aidan, before dropping off to sleep.

The following morning, Mother Jones made a welcome announcement. "Today we'll take a train to the next town. We've earned a break, haven't we?"

Aidan and Gussie shouted, "Yes, ma'am!" Neither had ever ridden on a train before.

At first Gussie and Aidan chased each other up and down the aisle. Once they'd had enough of that, they watched the passing scenery. It helped them forget how much they missed home and their families.

When they arrived, three thousand people were gathered in the town's public park waiting to hear Mother Jones speak.

"All these people care about us!" said an astounded Aidan.

Gussie was so amazed she could only nod.

Mother Jones spoke with force. "These children work twelve hours a day, six days a week. They work while other children go to school, play games and enjoy life."

Inspired, and maybe a bit humbled, many of the townspeople offered their support and places to stay.

Finally, a little over two weeks after the march started, the remaining thirty marchers arrived in New York City. It was their last stop before Oyster Bay.

Mother Jones was expecting to hold a parade through the city's streets and to speak at Madison Square Garden. But the mayor of America's largest city wouldn't allow her to do either.

Not one to take no for an answer, Mother Jones simply turned to the marchers and shouted, "Follow me, everyone!"

Stopping at the corner of 24th Street and 4th Avenue, Mother Jones held her meeting. More than a thousand gathered to listen, while the traffic whizzed around them.

After the speech, the group started to prepare for the last stretch of the march.

But Mother Jones had other plans. "Today, my friends, we're going to Coney Island!" she said.

Gussie gave Aidan a puzzled look. Aidan shrugged.

Coney Island was great fun. Aidan and Gussie ate foods they'd never had before — popcorn and peanuts and hot dogs. They went on rides called Razzle Dazzle, a circle that spun them dizzy, and Helter Skelter, a slide that took their breaths away.

They even saw two girls riding a camel!

Although it was a day for having fun, Mother Jones used every opportunity to speak out.

While Aidan and Gussie were looking at the wild animals, Mother Jones pulled them close and spoke to people who were gathered nearby.

"These children are as trapped as the animals in those cages. They are chained to the mills because they are poor and cannot break away. They suffer while you enjoy luxury."

These were hard words, but they were the truth.

The next day, the marchers walked the last thirty-five miles to Oyster Bay. It was a long, weary march, but finally they stood on the lawn of the president's summer home, waiting expectantly for him to appear.

But President Roosevelt wouldn't speak with Mother Jones.

"We've come from so far away!" said Gussie.

Aidan was angry, as well as disappointed. "How could he do that to us? It's not fair!"

Mother Jones put her arms around them. She could only agree.

On the train back home, everyone was quiet. Only Mother Jones understood what they had achieved with the march.

"Many people now see that children don't belong in factories and mills, but in schools," she reminded them. "Education will bring society closer to what we want — fairness for all and a better world in which to live."

Aidan thought about that. He was proud that he and Gussie had marched with Mother Jones. One day, he would learn to read, and when change came for mill children, he would be part of that, too.

Who Was Mother Jones?

On Our Way to Oyster Bay is based on a real person and a real event: on July 7, 1903, Mary Harris "Mother" Jones organized a protest march to demand an end to child labor. About two hundred adults and dozens of children walked with her from Philadelphia to New York City. Along the way, Mother Jones gave speeches and showed the crowds what working in factories and mills was doing to children, some as young as five years old. Aidan and Gussie are imagined characters that represent two of those children.

The march ended in New York City on July 23. Mother Jones, along with a few of the marchers, continued on to President Theodore "Teddy" Roosevelt's summer home on Long Island. After all their efforts, the president refused to meet with them. Although this angered the marchers, Mother Jones was satisfied that their protest had brought the issue to the attention of the nation. And in a few years' time, official laws against child labor were passed in Pennsylvania, New Jersey and New York.

Mother Jones began her life as Mary Harris in Ireland in 1837. She immigrated with her family to Toronto, Canada, when she was fourteen. Later, Mary became a teacher in Michigan before marrying a man named George E. Jones. After suffering a number of tragedies, including the loss of her husband and four children to yellow fever and later her home and dressmaking business to the Great Chicago Fire in 1871, Mary Harris Jones turned her pain into a passion for the rights of miners and their families. In June 1897, after she addressed a union convention, the miners began affectionately calling her "Mother."

Barely five feet tall, Mother Jones was a powerful speaker who told it like it was. She dressed all in black. She added years to her actual age — perhaps to seem more motherly and less threatening to the people in power. For the comfortably rich, or those whose wealth was gained through the hard work of the less fortunate, Mother Jones was, as the newspapers called her, "the most dangerous woman in America." For workers, however, she was a woman to celebrate. After her death in 1930, she was buried "with her boys" in the Union Miners Cemetery in Mount Olive, Illinois, where in 1936 the miners raised money to build a lasting memorial in her honor.

Child Labor Today

Mother Jones's march for children's rights may have happened over a hundred years ago, but child labor is not yet a thing of the past. Today, many millions of children around the world work in jobs that are harmful to their growth and development.

Child labor doesn't mean doing chores, such as making your bed or drying the dishes. It means work that children should *not* be doing because they are either too young or the work is dangerous and the conditions harsh. Children forced into labor can work such long hours, they are denied access to an education, as well.

Today, there are child laborers working in agriculture (for example, fish farming or harvesting cocoa beans used to make chocolate), manufacturing (for example, carpet weaving or

sewing soccer balls), mining (for example, working above and below ground in gold and salt mining), domestic service (for example, cleaning or cooking in someone else's home) and, dreadfully, wars (for example, carrying supplies or fighting).

In Mother Jones's Footsteps

Here are just a few examples of the many people who are fighting for children's rights today, with the same dedication as Mother Jones.

In 1995, twelve-year-old Canadian Craig Kielburger read about another twelve-year-old, a Pakistani boy named Iqbal Masih. After escaping the carpet factory where he had been forced to work under very poor conditions, Iqbal had become an activist, encouraging other children to escape. Horribly, he was murdered for speaking out against Pakistan's practice of bonded labor.

Moved by Iqbal's story, Craig got eleven friends together to form Free the Children, an organization that gives children the opportunity to help other children. Free the Children now has programs all over the world.

Kailash Satyarthi is also fighting to end child labor. In 1980, he founded the India-based movement called *Bachpan Bachao Andolan* (in English, Save the Childhood Movement). This organization's goal is "to create a child-friendly society, where all children are free from exploitation and receive free and quality education." Kailash received the 2014 Nobel Peace Prize, an honor he shared with Malala Yousafzai, who survived being shot when she was fifteen for speaking out in favor of education for girls in her native country, Pakistan.

Take Action!

There are day-to-day things you can do to help in the fight against child labor. For instance, when possible buy foods, including chocolate, that have Fairtrade, Rainforest Alliance and UTZ Good Inside symbols on the packaging. These symbols mean that the product was fairly produced without the use of child labor.

And there are many organizations, including the ones mentioned earlier, that accept donations to help in their fight against child labor. To raise money, you might get your friends, class or even your whole school together to hold a bake sale, car wash or yard sale. You can time your event around World Day Against Child Labor, which is celebrated each year on June 12. Or maybe for your next birthday or big holiday, you can ask people to give money to one of these organizations rather than buy you presents.

Knowing about this issue is a good first step toward stopping it. Here are some websites to help you learn more about child labor:

- Bachpan Bachao Andolan **www.bba.org.in**

- Free the Children **www.freethechildren.com**

- The United Nations Convention on the Rights of the Child (specifically Article 32) — in child-friendly language **www.unicef.ca/sites/default/files/ imce_uploads/child_friendly_crc_ncd_en.pdf**

- World Day Against Child Labor **www.un.org/en/events/childlabourday**

For Sylvia Lustgarten, whose heart is with the marchers — M.K.
For Emma — F.S.

Acknowledgments:
Thank you, Stacey Roderick, for inviting me on the march, for editing with grace and wisdom
and for finding the fabulous Felicita.

CitizenKid™ is a trademark of Kids Can Press Ltd.

Text © 2016 Monica Kulling
Illustrations © 2016 Felicita Sala

Kids Can Press acknowledges the financial support of the Government of Ontario, through the Ontario Media Development Corporation's Ontario Book Initiative; the Ontario Arts Council; the Canada Council for the Arts; and the Government of Canada, through the CBF, for our publishing activity.

Published in Canada by
Kids Can Press Ltd.
25 Dockside Drive
Toronto, ON M5A 0B5

Published in the U.S. by
Kids Can Press Ltd.
2250 Military Road
Tonawanda, NY 14150

www.kidscanpress.com

Edited by Stacey Roderick
Designed by Marie Bartholomew

This book is smyth sewn casebound.
Manufactured in Malaysia in 3/2016 by Tien Wah Press (Pte) Ltd.

CM 16 0 9 8 7 6 5 4 3 2 1

FSC
www.fsc.org
MIX
Paper from
responsible sources
FSC® C012700

Library and Archives Canada Cataloguing in Publication

Kulling, Monica, 1952–, author
    On our way to Oyster Bay : Mother Jones and her march for children's rights / written by Monica Kulling ; illustrated by Felicita Sala.

(CitizenKid)
ISBN 978-1-77138-325-7 (bound)

    1. Jones, Mother, 1837–1930 — Juvenile fiction. 2. Child labor — United States — History — Juvenile fiction. I. Sala, Felicita, illustrator II. Title. III. Series: CitizenKid

PS8571.U54O52 2016   jC813'.54   C2015-907020-1

Kids Can Press is a l'o̅rus™ Entertainment company

CURR
PZ
7
.K9490155
On
2016